DISCIPLES of TRIKAAL

PREQUEL STORY TO TIME TRAVELERS SERIES

VARUN SAYAL

ISBN: 978-93-5391-294-9

ABOUT
THE AUTHOR

Varun Sayal is a science fiction author who has built considerable repute in the writing world within a short span of time. His science fiction works, such as *Time Crawlers* and *Demons of Time*, have been phenomenal hits on Amazon. Testimony to that fact are over five hundred positive reviews on Amazon and other platforms within just months of publishing.

DEDICATED TO MY PARENTS;
I AM WHAT I AM TODAY,
BECAUSE OF THEM.
AND TO MY LOVELY WIFE,
WHO IS THE SOURCE
OF ALL MY STRENGTH
AND HAPPINESS.

TABLE OF CONTENTS

1

TRIKAAL

3723 BC, India

This was the seventh year of Aru's and Nemi's hard penance trying to please Trikaal Devi, the Goddess of Time. She was described in the scriptures as the eternal time traveler.

Both the men prayed atop the mountain peak Pulatsu. A saffron cloth called dhoti wrapped the bottom half of each of their bodies and was tied at the waist. Rudraksh necklaces adorned their frail torsos. Long-drawn beards now covered a large part of their faces and upper neck.

They stood on their left leg, with their right foot jammed at the back of their left knee. Their arms were stretched high above their head, their palms and fingers tightly interlaced into each other. Their eyes were closed and lips moved in the constant chant of only one mantra, *"Om Trikaal Deviyaye Namo Namah"*—Oh, Trikaal Devi, I salute you again and again.

Piercing raindrops from stormy clouds, scathing heat rays of the afternoon sun, and the harshest hailstorm of coldest winters could not deter their worship. Years of limited food intake had attenuated their once muscular bodies, but their spirit wasn't deterred at all. It was now a battle between the devotee and the lord.

They swapped the position of their legs every few months, which was when they also took some time to clean the plants growing on their feet and eat some food. The power of yogic life energy sustained them for the remaining time.

The fate they hoped for had eluded them for seven good years. But one day, they got what they wanted. They got the boons that changed their lives, and deaths, forever.

A thousand kilometers in the atmosphere, a bright circular surface emerged from nowhere. This vertically aligned circle's radius increased until it boasted a few hundred meters wide. The circle's periphery beamed with intense lightning while its surface was a dark blue viscous liquid—a wormhole from another world.

A small sphere made of flames shot through this wormhole like a blaze and traveled towards Aru and Nemi. It sped like a tiny meteor with a long smoky trail. It reached the mountain where they worshiped and zipped through the trees that surrounded them. The collision incinerated a few trees, igniting the rest on fire.

The sphere circled them a few times then slowly stopped. It floated in front of them for a moment, until they opened their eyes. Seeing the fiery sphere, they dropped onto their knees and clasped their hands in respect. Tears streaked their cheeks, and their throats were heavy with emotion. Their years of hard work bore fruit at last.

"I am Trikaal. Why did you summon me and force me to break my years of slumber?" The sphere varied its luminosity with each sound emanating from it. The voice resembled that of an old woman—graceful and decisive.

Aru shared a glance with Nemi then spoke in a humbled tone. "Oh, Goddess of Time, we worshipped you so you can give us your blessings and the boons we seek."

"I am not a goddess. I was human once. Millions of years of evolution introduced genetic changes into our species. We found a way to traverse time, to manipulate it, to inverse it. Before the universe went into the reverse crunch, we left our physical bodies. We all got together, joined our energies and now we are the travelers of the interstellar space. Together we formed the I, which I am now. I pass through time and other dimensions, like a man who walks a road. I am no god, and consequently, I offer no boons. The years you have spent worshipping me are as small as a flickering moment from my perspective."

Both men went silent. They felt deceived and angry. *What did she mean by 'no boons?'*

Nemi spoke this time. "The ancient scriptures say, when we worship you, you appear and give us what we want. They used the word *Trikaal Devi* for you—Devi, a goddess. Since you are here, that has to mean something."

The sphere spoke again. "The ancient sages who wrote those scriptures knew me well. They understood my powers. They summoned me and channelized me for the good of the world. They are the ones who documented the mantra, which is my invocation call. They used the word *Devi* out of respect, which your translation interpreted as *goddess*. However, I am not duty bound to serve your endless wishes."

Nemi's tone was rather insolent, and hence Aru motioned him to keep quiet. He addressed the sphere.

"We understand and respect what you said, Trikaal Devi. Our understanding of scriptures said that we get a *vardaan*—a boon. We seek to master time. Since your race mastered it, can you provide that knowledge to us?"

An uncomfortable silence followed. Aru and Nemi could hear their breathing.

Nemi was about to say something when the sphere again spoke. "I can guide you to master time. But each of you will have to choose one specific rule of time. Since this mortal coil cannot master all the rules of time, choose one."

Aru bowed his head. "If I have to choose one rule of time, I want the power to read time. I want to view the past, the present, and the future, whenever I want."

"I can teach you that."

Nemi donned a furious expression and muttered as discreetly as possible with little lip movement, "What the hell are you doing, Aru? Don't be a fool."

"I don't understand." Aru kept his face stoic, trying not to look at Nemi.

"You're asking for a power to just read time? What will you do all day, drowning in the dreams of archaic past and fantastic future? That's a huge waste of this opportunity. At least ask for the power of time travel. Don't squander this golden chance."

"Knowledge is what I seek, and this power will give me that. I am good with what I asked for."

"Suit yourself, fool."

"What about you? Which rule of time do you want to master?" The sphere addressed Nemi.

Nemi felt as if the sphere now regarded him, waiting. "I … I want to be immortal. Time should not corrode me."

The sphere shone more brightly as if a power surge afflicted it. It appeared the sphere was angry. "I cannot guide you to be immortal. That's the rule of time no one can break. Not even me."

"Why?" Nemi guffawed. He felt entitled to receive what he wanted.

"You were born. And that is why you must die. If you couldn't die, then you wouldn't have been born. Whatever starts, must end. The entropy of this world governs this cycle. You are bound to be dead by design."

"All right. Then give me the gift of time travel. I should be able to travel to the past and future." Nemi stood his ground this time.

The sphere paused for a moment before speaking. "Your body cannot not travel through time, but your consciousness can. You could possess the brain of any living organism in the past and the future. That's the only mode of time travel I can teach. Is that acceptable to you?"

"Yes, it is." A victorious grin floated on Nemi's lips, his brain already weaving scenarios of what all he could do with this immense power.

"Since each of us have chosen a rule, when do we begin our discipleship under you?" Aru's tone was humble.

"This body of flesh and bone is wasteful baggage which will impede your learning. In a few moments, you'll veer into sleep. Then I'll take your consciousness to a space called *Kaal-Shoonya*—the sinkhole of time. A small asteroid orbits this sinkhole, a place where time passes infinitesimally slower than on your planet. You will spend thousands of years on this asteroid, evolving yourselves. During this time, I'll engineer your evolution and ingrain the specific rules into your consciousness. Aru will learn time reading, and Nemi will learn to travel through time. When you're back in your bodies a few hours later, you shall have mastered what you wished for. And you won't remember anything from your time on this asteroid."

Aru and Nemi both smiled now. Though the entity in front of them was not calling it a boon, they were getting nothing short of one. With that, a sense of fear now creeped within them. Travel to a distant world, thousands of years of learning within a few hours—all these were inexplicable, unheard-of experiences.

"Before we begin our journey, you need to pay a price for what you're about to learn. When you return, both your lives will be locked together. Your time clocks will be coordinated."

Aru gulped. "What does that mean?"

"Your deaths will happen simultaneously. Death of one will invariably lead to the demise of the other."

"But if I can leave my physical body, I can't die. Can I?" Nemi half-smiled.

"You still can. At all times, you'll have to choose an anchor body. This body would be a starting pod for your time travel."

"So?"

"With the death of this mortal anchor body, your consciousness will extinguish as well. You will cease to exist."

Nemi's happiness was dimmed. But he had no choice. The way Trikaal put it, this clearly was a take-it-or-leave-it offer.

"Are you both ready to accept this price?"

Aru and Nemi nodded.

They then felt delirious and fell to the ground unconscious. The sphere's fire invigorated as it circled their bodies three times again and sped into the atmosphere. It raced to the wormhole and disappeared into it. The wormhole's viscous surface churned in circles as if a great force was sucking the liquid. The liquid disappeared into thin air. The bright periphery cracked into thousands of flakes of burnt ash and vanished into the atmosphere.

2
THE DELUGE

One year had passed since Aru and Nemi met Trikaal. After they returned to their bodies, they existed in a state of half-trance. Without exchanging words, they simply traveled back to their respective homes.

To the dismay of their families, it took days before they could eat and sleep properly and weeks before they spoke coherently. Around three months after their return, they returned to somewhat normal. Having no memory of what they had experienced at the asteroid, they remained clueless about their time spent near the sinkhole of time. But both were eager to test the extent of their respective powers. None of them tried to contact the other during this time.

Aru had spent the rest of his year regularly practicing his time reading. He started with simple visions of the immediate future, and each time what he saw came true. He envisioned the guests and beggars who would come to his house the very next day. He could predict extreme weather patterns with accuracy. He knew his wife, Rutuja, was pregnant even before she knew it. He also reviewed some visions in the past, who his forefathers were. All this while, he just served to gain more knowledge and satisfy his curiosity.

One fine morning, he sat in a garden Mehu-Vatika, teaching a few kids. His hair was trimmed, face shaved, and he wore a simple red dhoti. He covered his torso with a light red cloth. It was the beginning of the spring season, and a slight chill hung in the air—a reminder of the winter that receded a few days ago. Plants had blossomed with colorful flowers.

Aru sat on a large white stone with fifty or so children surrounding him on the ground, their eyes closed. He chanted verses, and they repeated after him. With a smile, he explained to them the meaning of the poetry behind each verse before moving on to the next.

As he took a deep breath, a sudden smell of wet mud filled his nostrils. He stopped his chant and looked skyward. The sun shone bright, and the sky was clear azure—not a hint of a cloud.

He stood and touched the earth. The ground contained moisture. This was strange for Aru. He knew that Mehu-Vatika was not a private garden, and the caretaker did not regularly maintain its upkeep. It was very unlikely the gardener had recently watered this zone.

Aru called Basant, Mehu-Vatika's sixty-something-year-old gardener who wore rugged dirt-filled trousers and a patchy shirt. He ran to Aru, holding moist mud. Basant confirmed Aru's doubt. He had not watered this area for the past several days.

With concern in his eyes, Aru thought of some possibilities and decided upon the most probable one. It must be the dam that controlled the flow of river Jhelputra.

Their village was nearest to the river, and this garden was only a few meters from the dam's base. Wet mud could only mean the dam had developed micro-cracks and that water had been seeping through the mud for the past few hours. Aru whispered his hypothesis in Basant's ear, who gulped in fear. Aru signaled him to stay quiet; he didn't want the kids to panic.

He canceled the rest of the lesson and asked the kids to return to their homes. Basant wanted to run through the village and inform everyone. Aru asked him to stay put. He knew others would not believe him just because they saw wet mud in the garden.

He sat on the stone and closed his eyes. While he focused on reading the next few days, Basant stood to the side, saying a silent prayer. The garden's tranquil environment boosted Aru's concentration and helped him float his gaze into the deepest recesses of time.

Though Aru's eyes were closed, Basant could see his eyeballs moving rapidly. Basant was afraid of the consequences of the dam rupturing, but he was caught in the curiosity of the moment. He knew Aru to be a learned guru who regularly taught village kids. *But what was Aru doing right then?*

Basant watched in amazement as Aru's facial expressions turned from a mild disquiet to anxiety. The wrinkles on his forehead deepened with each passing moment as his eyeballs fluttered. Basant gasped as tears appeared in Aru's eyes, and he sobbed.

Aru opened his eyes and stood. He felt weak in his gut and dropped onto his knees.

Basant's body trembled, his voice shaky. "What happened, Guru Aru?"

Aru's throat was heavy; he could only manage one word. "Deluge!"

The next morning, Aru sat in a rickety bullock-cart, treading the half-broken mud road which lead outside the village. While he drove the cart, his seven-months-pregnant wife, Rutuja, sat at the back asleep.

Rutuja wore a green saree with a maroon border, and red vermilion was smeared on her forehead where her hair parted. She wore no ornament except the thin austere necklace her father gifted her on their wedding. Alongside her rested their scant belongings—two pieces of rolled-up bedding, a few crumpled clothes, and old utensils wrapped in a large sheet of cloth.

As he drove the cart, his thoughts veered to the public disgrace he had faced in front of the villagers a few hours ago. No one had believed that he had seen the future. Some had called him a fool, some insane. One of the outspoken villagers had even called him an evil aghori—a necromancer, for predicting a fatal flood. Being the kind soul he was, their impending fate pained him more than his humiliation.

The bullock-cart wheel hit a sharp stone, and the cart shook violently. Rutuja awoke, cursing. "Be careful!"

Aru pressed his left ear with his thumb and index finger, signaling an apology.

Rutuja's sullen expression remained on her face. She was in her early twenties, but, whenever she looked in the mirror, she found herself aging fast. Her list of problems was never ending—advance stages of pregnancy, meager earnings Aru got from teaching village kids. Upon that, the village council had thrown them out of the village. *Where would we go now? My father won't let us stay with him. Not for long.*

Aru seemed unmoved. She had been beholding everything quietly, drinking all the anger within, until this day. Not anymore.

"You could have kept quiet about the flood thing." Her tone was caustic.

Aru gave a wry smile, knowing she was angry. "Those people will die. I had to warn them."

"Just because you saw a dream?"

"It was not a dream. It's the truth. I can see the past, the present, and the future. Did I not tell you about the baby two weeks before you knew it?"

"That was a fluke. And before telling villagers about your prophecy of the flood, did you not read the future that they will throw us out like stray dogs?"

"Rutuja!" Aru gulped. She had so much anger within her. "No, I did not see that, because the future changed the moment I decided to tell them. Even I am trying to wrap my head around this power. I do not understand it. I always understood time to be static, but now my simple actions change its flow."

Rutuja wasn't listening. She was least interested in her husband's strange theoretical concoctions. She mumbled in anger, but loud enough for Aru to hear, "My father said, he is a learned man. He will keep you happy. What a lie. All my dreams of having a good life have been swept down the drain."

Aru wanted to retort, but he kept quiet and drove. There was no time to stop and bicker. He wanted to cross the small forest in front of them before sunset and take refuge in the next village. There he could plan his next steps, away from the danger of flood and death.

3
FLIGHT 7E 449

It was a fine morning on seventh June, 2031 AD. Flight 7E 449 of Vontassia Airways had lifted off from the JFK two hours ago and was inbound to Narita, Japan. The seven-hundred-seater UF 880 wide-bodied plane was cruising at thirty-four thousand feet. Victoria Dunham and her co-pilot, Neil Dryker, sat talking. Victoria was eating a light meal.

At fifty years of age and thousands of flying hours under her belt, Victoria was a senior captain with Vontassia. She was routinely paired with younger pilots, such as Neil. She helped them gain more confidence in flying this gigantic six-hundred-ton aircraft.

UF 880 was a recent addition to the Vontassia fleet and one of the biggest aircrafts in the world, with a wingspan of three hundred feet. That's what made Victoria jittery as she planned to take a quick nap. Neil was to fly the plane alone for two hours.

As per new aviation rules, on long flights such as these, regulations did not require both the pilots to be present in the flight deck. They were only required for takeoff, landing, and emergencies. If a pilot was not fully rested from a previous flight, regulations mandated he or she to take some rest during a flight.

"So, I'll be back in two hours then?" Victoria wiped the edge of her lips with a tissue and thrust her plates in a disposable can attached to the wall.

"You don't sound too convinced to go take a nap." Neil nervously chuckled as he pressed a button to recheck their coordinates. He was a tall man in his early thirties with graying hair. "Are you not confident I can fly alone?"

"Nah. I know you're fully capable of not only flying but landing this beast alone. And the weather is largely clean along the way."

"I won't be worried if I were you, because A, I can handle it, and B, Tovi is gonna do most of the flying anyways."

They laughed together. Tactile Off-Ground Vehicular Intelligence, T.O.V.I. was the nickname for new aviation AI which had been powering the airplanes for last three years.

Victoria exited and closed the door behind her. She climbed the stairs and entered a cabin upstairs.

Neil sat relaxed as the computer screen in front of him displayed an array of metrics. He also received periodic feed from the air-traffic control towers they passed along the way. As he checked the console, he felt a sudden uneasiness at the back of his neck, as if an invisible hand lightly stroked him. His eyeballs had a slight pink glow, which lasted for a second. He inspected his hands and his dress. "Wow!" He curled his fingers into a fist and uncurled them. He repeated that a few times and chuckled each time.

He looked outside the window, and all he saw was the empty horizon. A thick cloud cover lay a few thousand feet below them. "This is amazing." For the first time, he noted the language he spoke and touched his lower lip as a reflex. "What language is this? English!" He was aflush with a deep sense of joy.

A knock on the door behind him caused him to unclick his seat belt and rise from his seat.

"Hello, Captain. Can I bring a food tray for you now?" a soft voice echoed from behind the door.

He paused and regarded the round doorknob on the metal door. He instinctively turned the knob and opened the door.

Young cabin crew Jennifer entered.

Neil closed the door behind her.

"Can I bring the food tray, Captain?" Jennifer was a sleek twenty-eight-year-old donning a warm smile.

"You're a beautiful woman, aren't you?" Neil gulped as his gaze froze on her, beholding her.

Jennifer realized he was gawking at her cleavage. "What do you mean?" she thundered. Being an airhostess, she had seen her fair share of flirty, obnoxious passengers who left no chance to take advantage. Passengers would intentionally brush past her, elbow her and stare at her body parts as she passed through the aisles. But her fellow male crew had largely been friendly and professional. She had flown with Neil a few times before and had known him to be a gentleman. His remark shocked her.

"I meant what I said." Neil licked his lips and eyed her body. "I'm new to this language and this body, you see. But I think I said you are a crafty piece of work."

Jennifer could feel tiny insects crawling under her skin. A coworker was violating her in the most unexpected places, and her first response was to remain motionless. Her frozen expressions turned into fury. Deep hatred she felt for such men was invigorated. She collected herself and pointed in Neil's face. "Keep your filthy eyes off me, pervert. You are in big soup. I'll report you as soon as we land."

She was about to open the cabin door when Neil caught her by the hair and pulled her head backward. "Where are you going? I'm thirsty. Let me quench my thirst first."

"Let me go!"

Just outside the door, her fellow cabin crew, Jemima, heard a muffled scream and approached the cabin.

Inside, Neil slapped Jennifer. She tumbled and fell sideways with her full weight. Her neck landed on an edge of the pilot console and instantly broke. She collapsed on the ground, lifeless.

Neil looked at her. "Now I can have you in peace." He unbuckled his waist-belt, but another knock came on the door. Neil was furious. He opened the door, and Jemima tried to rush in, but he blocked her way.

"Captain, I heard a scream." Jemima realized Neil was trying to obstruct her view and his waist-belt was unbuckled. Her facial expression turned from concerned to furious. "Let me in!"

Neil looked outside and saw the passenger aisles. "I didn't realize this carrier was so big."

"What?" Jemima gave a confused look, pushed him aside and hurried in.

Neil exited slowly, observing the aircraft in awe and surveying the lights on the ceiling. He noticed business-class passengers engrossed in watching movies, playing games, and some snoring. Behind him, he heard Jemima's loud cries.

A few passengers also heard the cries, approached the pilot cabin and gathered outside.

Ignoring the ruckus brewing behind him, Neil walked until he reached the economy class and saw the full extent of the aircraft. He stood there for a second. Most passengers were asleep. A few stared at him.

He heard a stern female voice behind him. "What the hell is happening?"

He turned to see Victoria pointing a small pistol at him. Jemima stood behind her, sobbing. The passengers witnessing this all stood stiff in fear.

On flights where the government couldn't put a dedicated air marshal, the airliner equipped one of the senior and trusted pilots with a firearm. As part of the anti-terrorism initiative, they were trained to deal with circumstances such as these.

"Victoria, right? That's your name? That's what this brain is telling me." Neil smiled and stepped toward her.

"Stay where you are!" She readjusted her grasp on her firearm. "What did you do to Jennifer?"

"Nothing. She is a beautiful woman. Not an old hag, like you." Neil took another step toward her.

"One more step and I'll shoot," Victoria yelled.

Jemima ducked and took cover. Passengers on the sides also tried to sneak behind whichever surface they could get.

"Go ahead. This isn't my body." Neil took another step.

Victoria aimed at his knee and fired. A loud bang echoed, and Neil dropped to the ground, shrieking in pain. A few economy passengers who had gathered behind him now ran back to their seats, causing a small chaos across the aircraft.

"Oh God, the pain is so real." Neil banged his fist on the floor as he trembled in pain and shock. He lay on his stomach, his knee bleeding and torn. The shot had ruptured his tendon, and the bullet had lodged itself between the bones, surrounded by burnt flesh.

Victoria's breathing was elevated. She routinely attended several hours of small weapon training every year but had never shot anyone, until now.

Neil raised his head at Victoria. "Time to change my vessel."

Victoria turned to secure the flight deck but halted. A slight pink glow flickered in her eyeballs. A wicked smile floated on her face. "Wow, this is so easy."

Neil was now unconscious.

Victoria saw Jemima cowering in a corner, trembling in fear. She shifted her weapon from her right hand to her left, approached Jemima and hoisted her by her hair. She jammed the gun's muzzle below Jemima's chin. "You were the one who stopped me from getting laid peacefully. You are the one who caused all this."

"No, please, no. Don't kill me. I have a ten-year-old. His name is Malik. He's a beautiful boy." Jemima repeatedly pleaded as tears streaked her cheeks.

"Shut up! Shut your mouth." Victoria dug the muzzle farther into Jemima's chin.

Jemima urinated.

"You filthy woman! I came here for some fun, and you ruined it. But I'll enjoy myself regardless. I can kill you right now, but I need you to make an announcement. Will you do that for me?"

Jemima nodded with her full strength.

Victoria released her.

Jemima grabbed the phone receiver fixed in an adjacent wall and stared at Victoria.

"Repeat after me. Dear passengers of flight 7E 449."

"D-Dear pa-pa …" Words skipped Jemima's tongue.

"Give it to me, you moron." Victoria snatched the phone from Jemima and commenced an announcement. "Dear passengers of flight 7E 449. Today is the last day of your wretched lives. Pray to whichever deity you want to, because this airplane is going down."

Victoria banged the receiver on the wall and aimed at Jemima's forehead. "This is for fucking up my getting laid plans." She shot Jemima point blank, and her brains spilled on the aircraft floor with some spatters on Victoria's face and dress. Victoria stepped aside, entered the cockpit and locked the door behind her. She glanced at Jennifer's corpse and smirked. "Some other time."

She pulled levers and pushed buttons on the cockpit panel.

"Permission denied," a mechanized voice echoed in the cockpit.

"What? Tovi, give me full manual control."

Tovi's mechanized voice spoke again. "The operation you performed two point three five seconds ago would have plunged this plane on a downward trajectory. Such an operation would have been a risk to the safety of this aircraft. Hence, I deem you unfit to fly. Consequently, I have initiated the lockdown protocol. We will be landing at the nearest airport shortly. I will be taking care of navigation and announcements. Please sit down in your seat and buckle your seatbelt."

"Oh really? Do you want to keep *them* safe? All right. Take this." Victoria aimed the gun at the aircraft's front window and fired multiple shots. The first bullet ricocheted off the glass, leaving a significant crack before lodging itself in the pilot console. But each subsequent bullet developed more and more cracks and the window shattered.

The cabin pressure broke as air inside was sucked out with a rush, and Victoria and Jennifer's bodies flew out like rag dolls. The plane shook vigorously and began a steep descent.

Nemi awoke in his bed, back in his body. He realized it had not been a dream. He had traveled to the future and returned. He moved his jaw several times and touched his face and shoulders, trying to assure he was back. He was still adapting to wandering outside his body and time traveling to other time slices.

His thirty-year-old wife, Kalika, sat next to him, smiling. Her dark red saree and long gold necklace accented her fair complexion. A thick nose piece adorned her face. She playfully ran her fingers through Nemi's hair. "What happened? You slept and woke up in a moment."

"It was more than a moment. I wandered off to the future." Nemi stood but felt weak in his legs. He approached the window and looked outside at the clear sky. "You won't believe me. I was inside a huge airplane."

"Airplane?" Kalika laughed. "I thought you were dreaming of me."

Nemi was still lost. "A huge carriage flying very high in the air, carrying hundreds of passengers." Flashes of what he did in the future came to him—possessing Neil and Victoria, firing gunshots. A strange smile floated on his lips. He was realizing the full extent of his immense power.

His abnormal expression worried Kalika. "Are you all right?"

Nemi studied her anxious face and softly held her shoulders to get her up. "You don't worry, my love. This power I have has turned me into a god. And wives of gods needn't be afraid of anything."

"You are scaring me, dear husband. Are you comparing yourself to the gods?"

"Not comparing." Nemi's eyes widened in wonder, and his jaw stretched in an insane smile. "I *am* a god."

Kalika gazed into his eyes and only saw pure madness. *What was this power doing to him?*

"When I enter another body, I absorb all its knowledge—its memories, learning, and languages. I know everything within a few moments. With this power, I could speak the language of the future, fire their weapons with ease. I knew exactly what to do and how to do it."

"Weapons?"

"Yes, my love."

"I am afraid that—"

"No! Don't use that word." Nemi placed his index finger on her lips. "They used their weapon on me. But it couldn't kill me. It hurt the body I occupied, my vessel. But I was unscathed. Your husband is invincible."

Kalika wasn't affected. "No, you are not!"

Nemi smiled. "I can leave the body whenever I want. Weapons can only kill the mortal body, but I am immortal."

"What about Aru?"

Nemi grinned. "What about him?"

"You said if he dies, you …" Her throat felt heavy. She could not bring herself to utter those words. "If something happens to Aru, what then?"

Nemi's mirth turned into nervousness. Kalika was right. Trikaal Devi's boon tied their deaths together. Even with the immense power bestowed upon him, Aru was now his biggest weakness. Restlessness surged through his body as he concocted a plan. "Don't worry, my love. I will fix him. But first, I need to do something far more important."

"What?"

He hugged her tightly and kissed her lips. He relocated his hands from her back to behind her thighs. He grabbed them and lifted her with his full strength.

She giggled.

He threw her on the bed and started to undress.

4
THE DECEPTION

ru stepped outside the small abandoned shack in the woods where he and Rutuja had spent the last three days, the first refuge they could find outside their village.

Rutuja had developed pain in the lower abdomen due to the strenuous bullock-cart journey. She refused to go any farther.

Aru gathered a few fruits from nearby trees and collected water from a small well near the house. He wanted to sit and time-read the village's present happenings, but his heart sank each time he recalled his previous visions.

He flung a metal bucket tied to a rope inside the well and used the pulley to hoist it out. As he transferred the water from the bucket into an earthen pot, he heard coordinated footsteps and the clanking of metal armor and froze.

Approximately twenty soldiers from King Varman's army marched toward the shack. Dressed in red uniforms and shining metal armor, their gait didn't look friendly. Before he could concentrate on time reading them, five soldiers broke their formation and approached the shack.

The rest of them kept marching toward Aru.

Aru threw the earthen pot and ran toward the shack. "No, don't go in there. Leave my wife alone."

Two soldiers intercepted him and clasped his arms.

He shook vigorously to get free.

A soldier struck his head with the butt of his sword, and Aru fell on the ground. His head felt heavy. Slipping into unconsciousness and through his blurred vision, he saw the soldiers dragging his wife from the shack. He made a feeble attempt to crawl in her direction before he blacked out.

He awoke in an unkempt hard bed—a cement block with a thin mattress—in a dingy jail cell smelling of sewer, rats, and dried blood. As he sat up, he still felt a mild concussion. He noticed a guard gawking at him from outside the bars. For the first time in years, he felt like cursing, but he didn't. He had taken a pledge of yogic meditation long ago. With that, he had to take an oath to control feelings such as anger and lust for worldly desires. This oath was essential for him to be a master of yogic science. But the circumstances made it difficult for him to keep his anger in check.

"He's up. Send a word to the king," the guard yelled at someone.

King? What does the king have to do with me? Though he decided not to speculate anymore, he knew how to get answers, by time reading. He was tired, hungry, and hurt, but his desire to know the condition of his wife propelled him. He sat down, closed his eyes and concentrated.

He saw his wife in a similar jail cell. He winced at the mere sight of her sleeping on the cement block, rolling over in discomfort.

He quickly focused on King Kumar Dev Varman, the ruler of the massive kingdom of Dev Nagar of which his village was a minuscule part. He was known among the masses as Varman. A fair king and a kind-hearted ruler, he cared for his subjects.

Aru reviewed the events of a few hours ago. The king rose in the morning, visited Queen Tejaswini, got ready and went to the court. Aru felt guilty canvassing the private moments of another person but skimmed over those quickly. He was not a voyeur, and he didn't intend to become one.

He glossed over the events of the court but couldn't notice anything unusual. The best part about time visioning was he could read the events at a thousand times faster pace without losing any information; he could read the whole day in a few minutes, and, if he skipped a few hours, he would be even faster.

Not finding anything in the immediate vicinity, he revisited the king's past three days—usual court routine, visited the queen in her palace, went on a hunt. *Wait a moment. Something happened there.* He slowed his time vision and replayed it.

King Varman was dressed in black armor and rode a horse while holding a spear. A long sword hung at his back, secured in a dark maroon sheath.

Varman, an experienced horse rider, carefully navigated through the forest. During his chase, his forehead bumped into a tree branch, and he fell from the horse. While he was concussed for a few moments, Aru saw a momentary faint pink glow in his eyes. After that, Varman stood, abruptly suspended his hunt and returned to the palace. The king usually had predesignated times when he visited the queen, but, as soon as he returned, he visited the queen and made love to her.

Aru paused. What was this magic? What was that faint glow? He focused on the glow's source and reversed the vision. The glow resulted from a streak of energy particles that originated from a gigantic black sphere very far away. Aru focused on that sphere, but just when he tried to look inside the sphere, he felt giddy.

The sphere was completely dark, but blazing light ignited its periphery. Aru realized this sphere was an astronomical body called a Shoonya—nothingness. Not even light could escape this enigmatic sphere. Guru Keshit had told him about these mysterious objects once. He didn't understand astronomy but learned these gigantic objects were formed after a star died.

Without focusing on the Shoonya, Aru followed the path of the streak of energy particles. He further reversed the time vision and tracked the particles' origin. What he saw next jolted him from within. All the puzzle pieces came together. The energy particles had originated from Nemi's forehead as he slept in his room. Nemi used his boon, his newfound power to not travel in time but to possess another individual—King Varman.

A loud clank of metal broke his concentration, and he opened his eyes. The same soldier glared at him. "I've been screaming at you, but you have not responded. Get up at once, you fool. His Highness the Maharaja of Dev Nagar, Shri Kumar Dev Varman is in your presence. Get up, and salute him."

Aru surveyed the king standing outside the jail cell donning a resplendent dress. Wearing a beautiful combination of the green velvety long robe with gold patterns, the king was adorned with shining jewels and a matching designer coat. Several priceless diamonds studded his heavy solid-gold crown. He stood there smiling.

Aru grinded his teeth but kept his anger in control. He wanted to have a hard conversation with Nemi. What he had done was unacceptable. They both were the disciples of the same guru. They had read the ancient scriptures together and worshipped Trikaal Devi together for years. And now Nemi was doing the unthinkable.

Aru bowed a little. "Please accept my greetings, King Nemi. Oh, forgive me, King Varman."

King Varman stood frozen. Aru had used the word *Nemi*. Varman loudly ordered, "Soldier, why don't you wait from me downstairs. I want to talk to this inmate in private. And don't allow anyone to come here until my next orders."

The soldier saluted and hurried away.

Aru waited for him to be gone and then banged the jailcell bars. "Why have you imprisoned me and my pregnant wife?" He wanted to stretch his hand outside and grab Nemi by the collar.

"Wow, you know everything?" Nemi smiled. Aru's powers both impressed and intimated him. "You time-read me, didn't you? But first, how do I look?" Nemi adjusted his crown and gave a furious smile, mocking Aru.

"Answer my question first!"

"Well, I brought you here for your security." Nemi made a fake innocent face. "Because I care so much for you, I have put you and your wife in my protective custody."

Aru smirked. "Lies. You've changed, Nemi. You're not the friend and co-disciple I once knew. Your power has corrupted you. You possessed the king, and you made love to his wife. That is rape. Using his power and influence, you captured me. What is your end goal here?"

Nemi took a deep breath and sat on a comfortable seat placed in front of the jailcell for him. "Aru, my friend. I just want to keep you safe, because if something happens to you, if you lose your life, the same fate befalls me. I, unfortunately, cannot afford that. I am realizing the vast extent of my powers, and I want to relish them for as long as possible. As for your allegations, I asked for immortality so I could conquer the world. Don't blame me for trying to fulfill my dreams."

"Your dreams?" Aru shook his head. Words skipped his tongue. He was now trying to think of ways to get from his grasp. He calmed down. "You want to keep me imprisoned. Do it. Please let me my wife go."

Nemi raised an eyebrow. "Umm, no. She's the only leverage I have on you. You know my secret. What if you tell someone? The moment you do. I will cut her into two pieces and—"

"Stop, please." Aru's eyes were wet. His once-trusted friend had turned out to be an evil now threatening to ruin his whole life. "Cut my tongue, okay? I won't tell anyone. Please let my wife go safely."

Nemi stood. "You know what? You can help me. My current travels to the future are rather blind. You can guide me to specific locations and times. I want to learn about the kings of the past and the future. I want to possess them and live their pleasure-filled lives."

Aru shook his head. "No, never. I will never aid you. You want to live their lives, but to what extent? Lust for power, money, and carnal desires has never fulfilled anyone. They are an endless abyss. With each misuse of your power, you'll become much hollower inside."

Nemi inserted his index finger into his left ear and shook it vigorously. "You sound an awful lot like our guru. That oldie used to kill us with his lectures on morality. Bastard would ramble for hours." Nemi spoke in a mocking voice. "Don't do this, don't do that. I was sick of it. I only studied under him so he'd give me the Trikaal Devi mantra. A few more days with him and I would have killed him in his sleep."

Aru kept silent. Nemi was beyond repair. He had burned his morals—or he'd had none from the beginning and only had pretended to be a kind soul. Aru was not sure anymore. Nothing he could say would change Nemi's heart.

"So, will you help me conquer the world?" Nemi asked. Aru was about to say something when Nemi interrupted. "We don't have to sort it out right now. You can think about it. I have a few important meetings to attend. My soldiers have acquired some damsels for my new harem. I must go check them out. And then my original wife, Kalika, will also join me as my new queen. Can't live without my first love, you see. Then I must find some innovate ways to punish the criminals captured for petty crimes. Loads to do and too little time. You and me, we'll keep talking." Nemi chuckled and walked away.

Aru sat on the cement block with his head tightly clasped in his hands. He was in a situation from which he saw no escape. He was worried for Rutuja and the baby who had not yet seen this world. Their lives were in danger, and he couldn't do anything about it.

Nemi walked outside the jail and sat under the shade of a tree. He had scoured Varman's brain for all his loyal subjects, and one name that echoed inside him was Giri.

Giri had been one of the best field marshals King Varman had, and he was an ardent loyalist to the throne. Nemi asked for Giri to be summoned to the jail at once.

After about two hours, a bulky man entered the jail compound and approached the tree where Nemi sat. At seven feet tall and sporting well-built muscles, Giri was no less than a giant. Varman's brain had all positive memories of Giri, but his muscular structure and stony facial expressions still intimidated Nemi.

What if he comes to know that his beloved king has been possessed by an impostor? Nemi couldn't even imagine what this beast could do with his bare hands. The thought that he could leave the body anytime was also not comforting him.

Giri approached him, kneeled and saluted to him. He spoke in a heavy coarse voice which suited his hefty structure. "Your Highness, you called for me?"

"Yes … I did," Nemi stammered, as he was still unsettled seeing the giant right in front of him. "Walk with me outside." He wanted to get out of this stinky jail compound at the earliest.

Giri walked beside him in a respectful stance. The king's security circled them in a defensive formation.

Nemi measured his words carefully. What he was about to say next was very important, but he did not want to raise any suspicion. "Giri, I have a very important job for you. This inmate I visited, his name is Aru. He is of special interest to me. I need him to be kept alive at all cost. If he is hurt, immediately attend to his wounds. If he refuses to eat, force feed him. If he falls sick, get him medical attention right away. I want him in good health at all times. No harm should come his way." Nemi paused. "Do you get my drift?"

Giri bowed his head. "Your orders are my command, Your Highness. I will guard him day and night with my life, and I will take all precautions. But what if he tries to kill himself?"

"Why do you say so?" Nemi removed a soft handkerchief and wiped the beads of sweat off his forehead.

"Your Highness, I have been hearing all kinds of stories about these jailcells. In this gloomy environment, some inmates try to end their lives."

Nemi was lost in thought as he chewed his lower lip. "You're right, Giri. Very smart thought. Do one thing, remove all unnecessary objects from his jailcell which he could use to hurt himself. And cuff him to the wall in a way that he cannot strangle himself."

Giri nodded.

"And yes, if he says something about me or tries to badmouth me, don't pay heed to him."

"You are my true king, Your Highness. No word above your word."

"Good." Nemi touched Giri's back in a patronizing way but quickly removed his hand. "Keep him sedated at all times. I don't want him to dream a lot and go mad."

Their voices faded as they walked outside the jail compound.

5
KRANTHIAN GLADIATORS

he Kranthian Empire reigned for four hundred years from 932 BC to 517 BC, after which it declined into ruins. At the peak of its influence, the kingdom stretched from the westernmost shores of modern Europe to the very end of the Hindu Kush in east Asia.

The kingdom's mega armies commandeered gold, silver, spices, and slaves from all newly annexed territories and sent them to the capital. The kingdom added new areas to its realm every few years.

On a fine morning, in the year 717 BC, the Kranthian King Waizeer the Third awoke an entirely different person. Nemi had possessed him—a kindhearted king morphed overnight into a tyrant who ruled mercilessly until his death. With his aggressive conquests, the cruel trouncing of rebellions and harsh criminal justice punishments, he wrote a gory tale in time. He entered the annals of history as one the worst despot to have ever ruled.

That morning, as Nemi stood at the topmost point of his castle and gazed at the vast expanse of the capital city, Kranthia, he licked his lips. His heart pumped with the possibilities of what he could do with King Waizeer's body. Hundreds of thousands of soldiers, numerous slaves, and endless treasures full of gold, silver, and precious diamonds were at his disposal. He was in for a mega treat for decades to come. He was about to create a heaven for himself and a hell for uncounted innocent men, women, and children.

"How long will this vessel sustain?" he murmured to himself as he observed Waizeer's, now his, muscular body in a large mirror. Faded scars from decade-old battles and smudged green tattoos of the gods were visible throughout his body. Though a forty-year-old, Waizeer looked much younger. His lavish yet well-maintained lifestyle had slowed his aging.

The day Nemi had chosen to possess Waizeer was on a special day called the Day of Redemption. King Waizeer, his clergymen, and several thousand Kranthians usually celebrated this day on the summer solstice and gathered at the special location called the House of Red. It was a day when the guards presented King Waizeer with special prisoners and he decided whether to punish or pardon them. These prisoners were men from tribes who had rebelled against his rule, but his soldiers had captured and transported them to the capital city.

House of Red was a gigantic oval stadium—seven hundred feet long and three hundred feet wide with a capacity of two hundred thousand spectators—visible from his palace window.

Nemi sneaked a glance at the city's skyline and entered his spacious bathroom where a hot water pool and a group of slaves waited for him. Soon after, he was to be decorated like a king and taken to the House of Red.

Capital city Kranthia was a remarkable metropolis, modern by the standards of that time. Aesthetically designed palaces, gardens, and fountains added to its beauty. A well-crafted road and sewage system made life luxurious for the men and women of noble descent who lived in the city. All the workers, servants, and men who did not belong to clergy lived in less affluent suburbs attached to Kranthia.

On Kranthia's southwest corner sat a vast barren land which the king had converted into a small town for slaves. Its population increased every year as Waizeer's armies crushed more rebellions on the outskirts of his empire. Soldiers sent more humans and materials to the capital.

In the middle of Kranthia stood the House of Red—a chosen spot for gladiatorial fights among captured slaves. But King Waizeer banned these fights three years after his father had crowned him the next king.

The king had converted the Day of Endless Blood into the Day of Redemption when he instead pardoned the rebels and gave them a new life. But that was about to change.

The crowd eagerly waited for King Waizeer. The mob erupted into cheers as he entered the stadium. They applauded as he approached his decorated throne at the other end via a special secured passageway. Armed security guards surrounded him in a coordinated gait. Chief Minister Marleek followed him religiously, trying to keep pace.

A noticeable hump afflicted the sixty-something-year-old Marleek. His head was bald; his eyebrows were white, and his face was crumpled with wrinkles. Nonetheless, he was the smartest man in Waizeer's cabinet.

He was a man with astute observation, and, since he had met with the king in the morning, he had seen a noticeable change in the way the king talked and carried himself. As a veteran politician, he loved stability and hated change. And he abhorred sudden unexpected changes. The king's behavior was a cause of big worry. Kings wielded near-infinite power, and small changes in their way of thinking could impact thousands of lives.

Marleek looked in wonder as Waizeer walked the secure aisle and waved to the crowd, donning a broad grin. The Waizeer he knew always walked straight with a nonchalant face. He rarely revealed his expressions to men. And he had never waved to the crowd. His cold demeanor reflected his absolute power. But today was a different day.

As Waizeer approached his throne, several ministers already sitting there rose and paid their respect. Waizeer nodded a little then sat on his ornate golden throne elevated on a high pedestal. Marleek sat at a distance on a much lower seat. The rest of the soldiers accompanying them stood guard at a distance.

Marleek waited for the crowd to settle then rose from his seat. He approached a special stage from where he would make an announcement. The engineers had acoustically designed the arena in such a way that any person speaking from this special stage would have his voice reach the whole stadium. To further augment the sound, five mammoth round metal cones sat at the bottom of this pedestal.

"Dear inhabitants of Kranthia," Marleek greeted the crowd with a broad smile. "I Marleek, the chief minister of King Waizeer the Merciful, welcomes you to the House of Red. And it's my pleasure to embark all of us upon yet another Day of Redemption. May we please bring all the men who have been placed at the mercy of lordship, His Highness, the first man of the kingdom, King Waizeer!"

A few claps and half-cheers emanated from the crowd. At the bottom of the stadium, the earth trembled as soldiers slowly displaced two heavy metal gates using ropes and levers. Armed soldiers thrust out several men from the gates and into the middle.

These men, once rebels, were the kingdom's captives and tied in iron shackles—more loosely around their feet so they could walk. Their ages ranged from fifteen to above sixty. They were tired, beaten, and poorly fed. Their clothes were disheveled and their faces bore looks of frustration, anger, and fear of the unknown.

Marleek waited for them to be in the middle of the stadium and resumed his announcement. "I now request His Highness to bestow upon these lost souls the benevolence of his big heart. He will now forgive—"

"Wait a moment!"

Marleek faced the king.

"I think we'll change things around here. Marleek, approach."

Marleek was half confused to leave the pedestal in the middle of the announcement, but the king's orders were ironclad. He climbed the stairs to the king's seat and waited at a distance. "Yes, Your Highness?"

"Let's give each of them a sword or spear or weapon of their choice. They all fight each other in this pit. Until death. And the one who survives will be declared the winner."

"But …" Words skipped Marleek's tongue. "My King, these are all men from the same tribe. There are fathers, uncles, brothers, and sons in there. They all know each other, have grown up with each other."

"So? That's the real fun, old man." Waizeer flashed a ravenous look. "Seeing them fight with each other, till death. Seeing them spilling each other's blood. I would love to witness that spectacle."

"As you wish, My King." Marleek's voice was shaky.

He was about to turn back when Waizeer spoke again. "Do we have big lizards somewhere in our kingdom?"

"Well yes, My King. Large Komodo lizards are found in the Mirbantia Desert, on our kingdom's southeast corner. They aren't poisonous but have been known to feed on cattle and men."

"Great. Let's arrange for few of them to be thrown into the pit with the men."

Marleek wiped the sweat on his forehead. "My apologies, My King. It will take a few months to capture and transport them here."

"Yes, I know. We will include them the next time. For now, let's go as is."

Marleek managed a fake smile. "Anything else, My Lord?"

Waizeer waved his hand.

Marleek bowed a little, turned back and returned to the announcement zone. He closed his eyes for a moment, silently sought forgiveness from the Lord Almighty and began his revised message, with a plastic smile on his face.

6
THE CONFIDANT

emi awoke in King Varman's body in his royal bed. He has been gone only a few hours in his own time, but he had spent twenty years ruling the Kranthian Empire.

Traveling back into time was tricky for Nemi, as he could never return to the same moment when he had commenced his travel. He was always off by a few hours. During the time he was out, he didn't want Varman to wake up before he returned. That could cause complications beyond his comprehensions. Hence, before his usual time travel, he would use a strong laxative to put Varman's body into a deep sleep. He then ventured out. This way, he was usually back before Varman woke up.

Nemi had also had his original body set on fire, the one in which he prayed to Trikaal Devi, the one in which he was born. Varman's body was his anchor-pod now, from which he commenced his time travel.

The few hours after he returned weren't easy for him either. He awoke tired and took some time to acclimate in the body he left.

This time too, after he came from Kranthia, he sat for a few minutes on his bed. He stood and walked around then again sat. When he felt comfortable enough, he clapped loudly, and a slave came in running.

"Send a message to the queen's palace. Tell my queen I want to meet her right away."

"I will call for Queen Tejaswini."

The slave bowed and was about rush out when Nemi cried out, "No, you fool! My new queen, Kalika Devi. Going forward, whenever I say *queen*, you understand what I am asking for."

Slave nodded several times and hurried away.

Soon after acquiring King Varman's body, Nemi had brought Kalika into the palace as his new queen. Several ministers advised against the practice of polygamy. Varman's first queen, Tejaswini, cried in front of him and spent days in a solitary room in mourning. But Nemi wasn't bothered with these trivialities. He was habitual of living with Kalika and wanted her by his side.

Nemi stayed in bed and ordered some fresh food for himself.

An hour later, Kalika arrived at the palace. As soon as she entered the room, she rushed and hugged him. "You were gone for so long, I was about to call the Aghori."

Nemi chuckled. "Why Aghori?"

"I don't know. I was worried."

"I came back from my travel. Before that, I was busy with some kingdom paperwork for two days. These stupid ministers won't let me go."

"These ministers, do they doubt your real identity?"

"One of them does. I've stopped meeting with him."

"And king's aunt, Induvati?"

"That old lady. I sent her on pilgrimage. She won't

return for six months." Nemi snickered. "So, as soon as I was done signing those useless sheets of paper, I went for my time travel. I confess to you, my love. I am getting addicted to it."

"Yes. Being the king is your new world. Plus, you love traveling to other worlds. Among all this, you have no time for your wife from your old world. I'm sure you've found a beautiful girl from another time." Kalika protruded her lower lip, showing fake anger.

Nemi pulled her toward him and hugged her. He whispered in her ear, "I have found some, no one as beautiful as you though." They then locked lips.

Kalika disengaged from him and wiped her lips. "You should rinse your mouth." She giggled.

"I am just back from my journey. Let me take rest." Nemi relaxed on the bed.

"No, you have to hurry up. We need to visit the temple."

"Temple, why? God is here. Right in front of you. Don't you go around pleasing the gods made of sand and stone."

"Nemi, my dear husband. You are going to be a father."

"What?" Nemi got up.

Kalika stood with her head down, her chin digging into her chest.

Nemi cupped her face with his hands. "Look at me. Is it true?"

Kalika nodded and blushed. "That's why I was so worried about you. You must be more careful with these time travels, Nemi. You have an additional responsibility now."

Nemi laughed uproariously. "Your husband is invincible, dear lady. Even death cannot touch me."

"Except …" Kalika chewed her lower lip. She hated to remind him of his weakness, but she felt it was her duty to keep him grounded.

The expression of mirth on Nemi's face slowly vanished. Kalika noticed wrinkles appearing on his forehead as he picked up a glass of wine and gulped it.

"Don't you worry about him." Nemi half-smiled. "I have that son of a bitch sedated at all times. He won't be able to do his time reading shit. He won't know what I am conniving. He will stay like that for the rest of his life. And, before he dies, I will live a thousand lifetimes." He downed the whole glass in one go. "Let me pay a visit to the poor bastard before I begin my next journey."

A few hours later, Aru awoke in his jailcell with a yawn. The effect of the mild anesthetic the guards administered every day was wearing off.

Giri's mighty shadow loomed in front of him with a plate of food. This was the daily routine followed twice a day. Giri would come in the morning and wake Aru. He then unshackled Aru and asked him to quickly clean himself. After which, Giri served him food and water. After Aru finished eating, Giri would pour a few drops of a black viscous liquid into Aru's mouth, and he would drift back into sleep.

On some days, Giri repeated this in the evenings too. On other days, Aru survived on a single meal. Giri thought that by following this strict routine of quickly administering the anesthetic, he was preventing Aru from meditating. That was exactly what the king had ordered, keeping Aru sedated. What Nemi and Giri did not know was that, in his sleep, Aru was still able to time read.

Like usual days, Aru cleaned himself and ate his food. He rinsed his mouth, after which Giri again shackled his hands and legs. Aru waited for Giri to pour anesthetic into his mouth, but Giri stood there waiting.

Aru was eager to go back to sleep and venture his thoughts to time reading. Though he at times veered to fantastic scenes from the future, he spent most of his time admiring his adorable newborn, Alek. He was sad that couldn't be near Rutuja when she gave birth and that he couldn't meet them. But he was content that his power allowed him to see them whenever he wanted. That could not quench his desire to hold his baby in his arms but was still better than nothing.

He regarded Giri with a questioning expression. "What happened, Giri, brother? You're not putting me to sleep today?"

"No. The king wants to see you. He'll be here any moment." Giri was stern and to the point as always.

Aru closed his eyes and relaxed.

"Open your eyes!" Giri thundered.

Aru was startled.

"The king has decreed against it. You only close your eyes when I give you the sedative. Understood?"

"Yes." Aru managed a feeble grunt. He was afraid of Giri, but he had been waiting for this moment. He wanted some talking time with Giri while he was awake.

Aru had been time reading Giri, and he had concocted a plan—a plan where, with the help of Giri, he could perhaps get his freedom. Though he knew it wasn't easy to make Giri pay heed to his words, so he wanted to make a short pitch, which not only would get Giri's attention but also rile him up.

Aru sat on the cement block and took a deep breath. "Your son. Nagesh. His life is in danger." There. Aru said it with all the courage in his body.

"What?" Giri frowned. "Are you threatening my son? How do you even know his name?" Giri no longer stood in a comfortable pose. He faced Aru as if about to pounce on him.

"No, I am not threatening him. I am saying what I saw. I'm a time reader. That's how I know his name. There will be an animal attack, five days from now."

"What are you blabbering, you son of a bitch? Have you lost your mind?" Giri was trying very hard to control himself. The king's strict orders were that no harm should come to Aru. But his words caught Giri's attention, in a wrong way.

Aru realized Nemi would be there anytime soon. He wanted to complete his pitch before that. This was a now-or-never situation. But he also feared backlash from Giri for what he was about to say.

He summoned all his courage. "Five days from now, when Nagesh goes to play in the field with his friends by the river, a jaguar will approach the them. Children will run, and the jaguar will chase. Your son being the youngest won't be able to outrun others. And ..."

"And what?" Giri almost screamed, his heartbeat skyrocketing.

Aru gulped. "The jaguar will drag him away. He'll never return."

Giri could no longer control himself. He clasped Aru's neck and, with his full force, lifted him above the floor.

Aru flailed to get free and struggled to breathe. "You ... can ... save ... him."

Giri threw him on the floor and turned his back, his muscles tense.

Aru lay on the ground coughing and catching his breath. When he could finally speak, he reiterated, "It's true, what I said."

"Not another word!" Giri pointed his finger at Aru. "The king was right. He told me not to listen to your deceiving words."

Aru stood and straightened his dress. He was still uneasy, but he had to win Giri's trust at any cost. The nail was dug into the wood; he just had to hammer it more.

"You were born exactly thirty-five years, three months, and twelve days ago. Your mother died three hours after your birth due to a heavy blood loss. You fell from a horse when you were seven years old, and a sharp stone edge sliced your face. That's how you got that scar."

Giri's hand instinctively touched the old scar on his cheek.

"When you were fourteen, you lost your father to the green fever. At twenty-five, you got married to a girl, Trishna. At twenty-six, Nagesh, your first child, was born, and two years back, at thirty-three, you had your daughter Kamla. Do you want me to continue?"

Giri felt as if his anger had slipped away. Aru had got these details with an exactitude. But he would not trust this prisoner so easily. "So what? A few people in my village knows these details. Have you sent spies after me?"

"Okay. I will come to specifics then. Yesterday, while you attended to your garden, a small baby snake jumped on you. Instead of killing it, you let it go." Aru eyed Giri.

Giri donned a grim expression. A snake did attack him the previous day. He was alone at that time, and he hadn't told anybody about the incident.

"This morning, when you woke up, you had a slight pain in your left foot, and you rotated it three times. You went to wake up your son, but, when you tried to hug him, he whispered in your ear that you stank of sweat. Then you stepped out of the house and almost slipped—"

"All right! Enough. Are you a sorcerer or a necromancer?" Giri had no reason not to believe Aru now, but his trust in Aru stood on shaky ground.

Aru heard footsteps at a distance, outside his jailcell. Nemi was close. Aru spoke in a hushed tone. "You know what, Giri? I've told you enough. It's up to you to believe me or not. My advice would be to not let your son go out that day. Don't let any of the kids go out that evening, five days from now."

Having heard the footsteps, Giri too whispered back, "Yes, you got a lot of things right. And I want to believe you, but how do you know all this?" Aru's prophecy about his son had him worried, and he wanted to believe this prisoner after all. But he was not a strong believer of the seers and the paranormal.

"I can see the past and the future. That's the truth. Let me offer a final proof for you. When the king comes here, he will dismiss you. His first sentence to me will be, 'How are you, my dear brother?' See if I get that right."

Giri nodded and stood aside.

King Varman appeared at the jailcell door, smiling. "Giri, will you give us a moment? I want to talk to the inmate alone."

"Yes, My King." Giri approached door, opened it and stepped outside. He locked the door from the outside, bowed to the king and started walking. *Aru was wrong. The king's first words were different. He* is *a charlatan after all.* Giri smirked as he walked away.

Nemi waited for Giri to be at a distance then addressed Aru. "How are you, my dear brother?"

Giri was a distance away, but he heard it. *Aru was bang-on right again. But how?* Giri's breathing became uneasy, and his heartbeat fluctuated. He wanted to return right away and ask Aru how he knew that, hut he kept walking until he disappeared into another alleyway, away from the king's gaze.

Inside the cell, Aru shot back at Nemi, "Don't call me *brother*. You're not doing anything brotherly by keeping me and my wife separated and imprisoned." He was careful not to mention his newborn. He wanted to maintain the impression he wasn't time reading anymore. The less Nemi knew, the better.

"Imprisoning you is self-preservation. You stay safe, I stay safe. It's as simple as that." Nemi grinned. "Nothing personal against you. I still consider you my family."

Aru snickered. "Family? You are nothing to me. I will never have any relation with a demon like you. Karma will catch up with you soon. You'll meet a fate that befits your actions. Humans may not know what you are, but almighty God he sees everything."

"Sometimes I feel there is no God. At other times, I feel I am God. I'm still divided between these two points of views."

Aru wanted to curse and scream. He hated the man in front of him with every muscle in his body. "Do you think you're the first person to have gotten the power of time travel? No. There have been numerous time travelers in history before you. Many of them utilized the power for the benefit of mankind. They were the saviors, the messiahs who reincarnated in new bodies again and again. With the immense knowledge and wisdom they gained in multiple lives, they led people on the path of fulfillment and prosperity. And then time travelers such as you exist, who possess others for power, wealth, carnal pleasures, and bloodlust. Your ilk is aptly called the Demons of Time."

Nemi stood stung for a moment then smiled. "Demons of Time. I like the sound of it. But let's talk about you, the intelligent one, the clairvoyant. You think you're so smart, don't you? Let me ask you something. You know so much about so many things. You can see the past and the future. Why did you not see me coming? Why did you not use your power?"

"Because I wasn't looking out for myself. I wish I had. But I was too concerned about others, about saving my village from a flood."

"See, that's the major difference between us. It's not our powers. It's our life goals. With your power of clairvoyance, you could have been a god too, like me. But you were foolish enough to indulge in the same boring life. And with that, you took upon yourself a goal of public welfare. Your village got flooded, by the way. Hundreds died. Someone from your village came to my court for help. I spat in his face and kicked him out." Nemi laughed loudly and clapped.

Aru restrained himself from yelling. "At least tell me about my wife. Did she give birth to a healthy baby?"

"You aren't time reading, are you? She gave birth to a boy. She named him Akhil or Alik, something like that. Don't worry. She's all good. I'm taking good care of her."

Aru was aware of the hardships his wife endured in the dingy house Nemi had placed her. She even developed an infection after childbirth due to its unhygienic surroundings. He drank all the anger he had for Nemi.

"Thank you for that." He pushed out those words without moving a muscle on his face.

"No problem. It's the least I can do. If you keep your mouth shut, they stay alive." He paused and eyed Aru. "The day you do something stupid, I promise I'll slice them myself."

A shiver ran down Aru's spine. He had already opened his mouth, confided in Giri. He was silently praying Giri kept his mouth shut.

Nemi clapped his hands and shouted, "Giri!"

Giri came running and stood in front of him, head down.

"Our inmate is not giving you any troubles, is he?" Nemi tilted his head as his gaze bore into Giri's eyes.

Giri glanced at Aru.

Aru felt his last breath was still stuck somewhere inside him. *Don't say anything, Giri. For God's sake, I trusted you.*

"No, My King," Giri said with confidence.

Aru breathed a sigh of relief.

"I am not giving this bastard any chance. He's only awake for food and ablutions. Your orders are cast in stone. I will never dare sway from them." Giri bowed a little.

Nemi patted Giri's large shoulders and smiled. "Well done, my man. Keep at it. Time to give him his dose."

Giri unlocked the jailcell and entered. He grabbed the small earthen pot kept on the side and signaled Aru to lie down. Aru sat on the cement block and laid down. Giri poured the liquid inside his mouth. Within a few seconds, Aru was knocked out.

7
STARSHIP RESTORATION

The year was 2196 AD. Multiple retro-virus pandemics and repeated ecological disasters had eradicated most of the Earth's population. The last global outbreak of the Vittaza virus in 2165 had reduced the human population to one and a half million. These survivors lived in a small quarantined colony thirty feet beneath a flat plateau next to the Himalayas. This colony, which spanned two acres and went several hundred levels underground, was called Ajeevam—Sanskrit for *lifelong*. All areas outside Ajeevam were declared a red zone, and no one ventured from its boundaries.

To make matters worse, the last remnants of the once-thick ozone layer had depleted to zero in the past five years. So, the Ajeevam inhabitants mostly stayed indoors. They could only venture outside in heavy protective suits. With inner greenhouse vegetation and lab-synthesized meats, the resources were scant, and life expectancy was low.

Over the past decade though, the death rate had stabilized. The human species was adapting, and the colony was slowly flourishing. The space exploration technology had peaked several decades back. With the solar-powered rockets, these survivors could send manned as well as unmanned probes into space every year.

Using satellites, they constantly searched for other livable areas throughout Earth. They also kept studying weather patterns and hunted for any other signs of life. Occasionally, they also launched small spaceships, which they called *starships*, for that's the name that had stuck throughout the centuries.

Starship *Restoration* was sent to space for a period of two years, and their mission was space scavenging. They were required to search for old discarded satellites orbiting Earth and salvage them for resources, such as metal or any working equipment. By the end of their mission, they were to collect the salvaged metals together in the form of a secure package and bring it back to Ajeevam.

Aboard the spaceship was a sparse crew of three people. The ship's captain was Namita Charles, a veteran astronaut. Two trained astronauts and scientists, William Cordow and Volga Pritok, were also aboard. All three mostly stayed inside the ship where the cabin was temperature and pressure controlled, so they wore normal clothing.

William and Volga were both proficient in scavenging metal from ships. They worked on magnetizing it so it stood together as a round metallic bundle as they keep adding more metal to it. Captain Namita was an expert in space navigation. She made sure the ship avoided collision with old satellites, small meteors, and other space objects as it orbited Earth, collecting trash.

Jim and Volga were in their early thirties. Namita turned forty-five the day *Restoration* took flight. She had not seen her family for nineteen months now. They still had five months left before they'd begin their slow descent toward their landing pod in a large lake fifty kilometers south of Ajeevam.

They had to be extra careful with the descent because they expected to collect around five tons of scrap metal by the end of their mission. That package would be tagging along as they returned. Any incorrect calculations and they risked landing the spaceship and the metal package right on top of Ajeevam. If that happened, they would crash into the colony, causing loss of lives and irreparable damage to the colony structure. Landing far from the colony was out of the question, as they would be in the red zone, so the calculation were to be precise. They had already collected about four ton of useful metal, so they were on track to meet their target.

Namita sat brooding about her family when Volga's voice broke her chain of thoughts. "Why so greedy, Billy?" Volga always called him Billy, though he insisted he is called William. "That's a massive piece. Better cut it into two halves and pull them one by one. Please?"

"You are so risk averse. We can pull it in one go." William carefully moved the thirty-foot-long robotic arms which outstretched from below *Restoration* to a small junk satellite. The rear end of these arms had industrial lasers. William used these to cut through the junk with finesse, separating clean metal from damaged pieces.

"If you pull a bigger one, you risk pulling the whole satellite toward us. How many times do I have to repeat that?" Volga faced Namita. "He's doing it again. He did this last week too." She spoke like a child complaining about her sibling to her mother.

Namita enjoyed their mild banter. At times, that was the only thing that kept her sane at the altitude of thirty thousand kilometers. But their work needed precision and careful attention. As ship's captain, she was duty bound to enforce the professionalism required to do their jobs.

"William, remember the little chat we had last time? You two are the only ones who can keep each other in check. We've been careful the whole—"

"The whole nineteen months, why get edgy now?" William mocked as he completed her sentence. "Yeah, yeah. I remember it, ma'am. I'll be careful."

Namita let these small jibes slide. Not everyone was built for long space trips. They were floating all the time. There was no sense of night or day. Food was crappier than usual, and no warm bed waited for them at the end of the day.

As Namita smirked at the repartee of her colleagues, a light pink glow flickered in her eyes. She took a deep breath. Nemi had arrived.

She surveyed her hands and clenched them into a fist. Nemi was testing her reflexes and reading her brain. He did this every time he took a new host.

He studied the spaceship's interior—buttons, levers, cabinets all along. He looked outside the window and observed the sun and the stars.

"Wow, this is another flying carriage," Nemi muttered. "Why do I always land in one of these?"

William and Volga didn't listen to him. They were about to finish the crucial task of separating the salvageable metal and were glued to their screens. Their backs were toward Namita.

Details from Namita's mind slowly came to Nemi. He spoke again, this time loudly. "This is … Starship *Restoration*. Nice name."

"Yeah, thanks for reiterating that, Captain Obvious." William chuckled, still engrossed in his work. He whispered to Volga, "Do you realize the pun here? She is the ship's captain as well as the captain obvious. Is it an example of a pun or something else?"

"Shut up, Billy," Volga snapped. "Please concentrate."

"Yeah, yeah, y'all need to lighten up a little."

Nemi approached the ship's console to study it. He whispered to himself, "I need to go to the planet and enjoy its riches. But how do I land this thing?"

Back in the jailcell, Giri splashed a bucket full of water on Aru's face. He lightly slapped Aru a few times.

Aru awoke startled. "What happened?"

"You saved my kid. You saved him!" Giri hugged Aru tightly, tears in his eyes.

Aru was still coming to his senses. "Okay, what time is it? Is it day or night?"

"Night, my friend." Giri wiped his tears. "This evening I asked the community to not send the kids for play. I told them a jaguar was prowling. Some folks listened to me, some didn't. A few kids went to play."

"I know." Aru's face was sad. "I saw it. One kid never came back." He had time read the outcome in his sleep.

"Yes, yes. But my son, my Nagesh, he is safe. All because of you. You are now my brother, my family, for life. Tell me what I need to do for you."

Aru paused. He wanted Giri's help but not at cost of this soldier's life. He was just following orders. "I won't ask you to free me, because if you do, Nemi will kill you."

"Who is Nemi?"

"Doesn't matter. I need two things from you. One, you have to find my wife and my baby boy and get them as far away from here as possible."

Giri touched his chest as if taking an oath. "Consider it done, brother. What's the second thing?"

"Promise me, after listening to my second ask, you won't say *no*." Aru now took Giri's hands in his own and clasped them.

"I take an oath brother. I will fulfill your ask within the best extent of my resources and efforts."

Tears filled Aru's eyes as Giri looked at him in anticipation.

On Spaceship *Restoration*, William pushed the final few buttons. "There we are. Done." He relaxed into his chair.

Volga too sat back. They had finished their jobs using the lasers. Now the robotic arms were attaching themselves to the broken metal and pulling it toward the metal package they already collected. Volga turned back and was surprised to see Namita staring at the ship's navigation console in a half-confused state. "What's happening, Captain?"

Namita looked at her but was still confused. "I know how to land this thing, but why is this brain advising me against doing so?"

Volga chuckled. "Stop joking, Captain."

William turned and stood. "Wait, Volga. I think the

captain is testing our classroom training. Let me take this one." He closed his eyes and reiterated from memory. "We need *Restoration* to be in the right position in the geostationary orbit if we need to land with preprogrammed safe descent. If we land from any other location, we will approach at the wrong speed and an incorrect angle. The coordinates would be Ajeevam, but we will come down crashing. Phew. I remember it exactly how they taught us in the class." He smiled with pride and pressed his index finger to the side of his forehead.

"*Come down crashing?* I like that," Nemi mumbled and grinned, showing his full teeth.

Volga and William could not understand the meaning of this uncanny smile. They had never seen Namita smile like that.

Nemi pushed the two red buttons on the main console and quickly pulled down one of the metallic levers from bottom to the top. All the lights inside the ship reddened.

"What are you doing?" Volga screamed.

Volga and William rushed to the console. They knew Namita had instructed the ship to take an immediate descent path to Earth, but they did not know how to undo it. The ship hadn't started moving yet though.

"We'll crash land. Thousands will die. Why did you do that?" William confronted Namita.

But she stood wearing a calm expression.

A mechanical voice echoed inside the ship. "I am *Restoration*, this starship's AI. You have engaged the starship to follow and immediate descent path. This course of travel has ninety-nine point nine-nine percent probability of a disaster landing. The descent will start after ninety seconds. You have time till then to disengage."

A reverse countdown of ninety seconds illuminated the screen.

Back in the jailcell, Giri stood in front of Aru. He held a small metal glass in his left hand. His forehead was beaded with sweat, and his hand trembled.

Aru exhibited a serene calm on his face.

"Are you sure, brother?" Giri's voice was gloomy.

"Yes. This is the only way."

Giri nodded and handed the glass to Aru.

"Are you sure this will work?"

"Yes. The snake venom will take a few seconds, but it should do."

Giri was almost in tears. The angel who saved his child, the one whom he now loved and respected as a brother had asked him for the impossible. "No chances of survival?"

Aru chuckled.

Giri shook his head. His lips pressed together. He was trying hard to not cry, but tears rolled down his cheeks. His grandfather told him to never send away a person crying, and he was trying his best.

"Remember your other promise. You're the only hope for Rutuja and Alek." Aru put the glass to his lips and drank the whole liquid in one gulp. He handed the glass to Giri and sat on the cement block. "Nothing is happ—" He convulsed and fell to the floor, a white froth emanating from his mouth.

Giri rushed to him and took him in his arms, but he couldn't do anything. He sobbed silently as Aru flailed, struggling for his life.

In *Restoration*, Namita and Volga scuffled while William frantically sifted through a thick paper manual. He had a hard time reading the small font text in the cabin's dim red light. The countdown on the screen read, *17 … 16 … 15 …*

Namita suddenly stopped fighting and disengaged from Volga.

"What happened?" Namita screamed; Nemi was gone, and she was still trying to recollect her senses.

12 … 11 …

Volga pointed at the console. "Stop this!"

Namita looked around and quickly floated to the console.

9 … 8 …

She rapidly pressed a few buttons and set the lever back into its original position.

5 … 4.

The countdown paused at 4. The cabin lights returned to normal. All three crewmembers could hear their heavy breathing. The danger was averted by a very narrow margin.

Nemi awoke in Varman's body. Gasping for breath, he couldn't understand what was happening. He too experienced convulsions. He fell onto his knees and crashed into a metal table nearby with a loud bang, spilling wine glasses and fruits.

A slave stationed outside the room heard the loud noise and came running. He looked in shock as the king lay on the ground, his body in a grand mal seizure.

"Call my queen … my Kalika."

The slave ran toward the door, but he stopped himself as the king now lay motionless. The slave sat and, with a trembling hand, checked the pulse. None. He rushed outside in a panic.

EPILOGUE

After King Varman died, Kalika was not allowed to stay in the capital, as she didn't belong to the royal descent. She left the kingdom and returned to her village house where, after a few months, she gave birth to twin boys. She named them Kumbh and Vetri.

Aru's sacrifice didn't go to waste. He had beset a demon and saved countless lives.

Giri stayed true to his promise and took Rutuja and her baby, Alek, to a safe location. With the king dead, the whole kingdom was thrown in a power tussle. Giri didn't have much difficulty rescuing Aru's family. Later, he also left the kingdom with his wife and children and went far away.

Starship *Restoration* completed its mission and returned safely to Earth. It transported more than five tons of precious metal. The crew remained completely clueless to what had happened that day. The medical staff checked Namita. They attributed her behavior to a random episode of temporary insanity. Ajeevam's leadership immediately discharged her of her duties and put her under medical observation for indefinite period.

Ten years had passed since that day. One morning, Kalika visited the Ashram of a sage, Kapitar. She had heard Kapitar was a seer and could read the future, so she visited him along with her kids. A question had been eating her from the inside, and she was in desperate need for an answer.

She sat inside an attic while Kumbh and Vetri played outside with other Ashram kids.

Kapitar was an eighty-year-old man with a frail body. He had a thick white mustache and beard and wore a saffron attire. He sat in front of her on a high pedestal with his eyes closed. She could see his eyeballs moving from one side to the other.

Kalika stood and glanced outside the window to assure Kumbh and Vetri were still playing in the Ashram's playground and had not wandered off. She returned and sat again, waiting for Kapitar to open his eyes. After a moment of tapping her feet and looking around, she got frustrated. "Guru Kapitar, it's been a long time since I—"

Kapitar sternly signaled her to keep quiet but kept his eyes closed. He opened them after a few seconds. "Your husband was a monster, a mass murderer. And you supported him? Why?" The sage was fuming.

"I …" Kalika stuttered. "He traversed his own path. I didn't know what he did with his powers."

"You knew everything. He told you everything."

"He was my husband, like a deity to me. It was not my place to question him."

"You could have …" Kapitar was furious, but he knew arguing with her was futile. "What do you want from me?"

"I heard you are a seer, you make prophecies."

"I am a time reader."

"Like Aru?" Kalika's forehead contracted in anger.

"Yes. But I am not as unfortunate as Aru. He had to sacrifice himself to save countless others from your husband."

"So, it's true my husband died because of that stupid Aru."

"You are calling *him* stupid?"

Kalika suppressed her anger. She realized she needed Kapitar's help with her impinging question. She touched her forehead to Kapitar's feet. The sage's hand raised in a blessing as a reflex.

"Guru Kapitar. I am ashamed of what my husband did. You're right. In part, I should be held accountable for what he did. But now I am worried about my kids. Kumbh told me yesterday he has been having a strange dream every night for the past few days. Sometimes he is flying in the sky, sometimes he is in strange places he has never visited. What is all this?"

"He has inherited the power of time travel—your other son, Vetri, too. What they see at night are not dreams. They are venturing from their bodies to other time slices. They are still kids, so these powers are not fully developed yet."

Kalika was grim. "So are their deaths tied to some other people too, like Nemi's death was?"

"No. Your husband was given a boon with a special death condition. Your kids are free of that."

Kalika couldn't hide her smile. "Thanks, Guru Kapitar. I will now take your leave." She turned and headed for the exit.

"I need to say something to you before you go." Kapitar stood from his seat.

Kalika stopped walking but didn't turn around. Her anger slowly returned.

Kapitar thought for a moment then spoke. "From our perspective, the future is tumultuous, always flickering with possibilities. I can see multiple futures happening. Your kids, they have a superpower of time travel. But how they use it is still undecided. It depends on you how you mold them and shape their thinking. Depending on the values they get from you, they will either be the angels or demons of time."

She turned back fuming. "My only teaching to them would be that they be very cautious of a certain type of human beings."

"Which type?"

"Time readers."

Kapitar wasn't amused. "I didn't expect a different answer. You will fill them with the same rage and blood-lust which your husband had. Don't expect a different outcome." Kapitar closed his eyes. "Although, one of your grandchildren will be different. Though a time-demon, he will be a kind soul who will always do good for mankind."

Kalika clenched her teeth, her face red with anger. "I won't let my children or grandchildren engage in the stupidity of thinking about the welfare of others. They will only think about themselves. They will live and rule like emperors."

Kapitar sat down with a serene calm on his face. "Multiple choices lead to similar outcomes. You can only control your decisions. You cannot control their consequences, only gods can."

"I may not be a god, but my sons will be." Kalika stormed from the room.

TO BE CONTINUED

LOVED THE STORY?
WANT TO READ FURTHER?

THE SERIES CONTINUES WITH

DEMONS OF TIME:

TIME TRAVELERS BOOK # 1

SOME REVIEWS FOR
DEMONS OF TIME

I was hooked from the very start and kept interested through the entire book. I recommend this book to readers that enjoy traditional quest stories but are ready for something new.

~ Karen Siddall

The story begins with the atmosphere of a fantasy novel and quickly lets you know that you have to do with people who are not in the least primitive. This is a great book and I cannot wait to read the next installment. Varun is a force to watch on the science fiction scene.

~ DDBookReviews

This book is fantastical woven with science fiction, fantasy, Hindu mythology, and more. The cover is awesome! I am early waiting for the next book in the series. I would recommend this book to all science fiction and fantasy fans.

~ RM Griffin

An enjoyable and fast paced novella, ... blends a lot of sci fi with a bit of fantasy magic. There are characters to root for (and against), and more than enough action and adventure to make this worth a read!

~ Justine K. Barr

What I really enjoyed about this book was the vast world that Sayal has created. ... immersed in this world of time travel that Sayal has created. You'll fall into Tej's world, holding your breath as he fights to save humanity. Packed with rounded characters and plenty of twists and turns, this book works well as an introduction to what looks like a new series. If you're looking for something different and out of the box, definitely check out Varun Sayal!

~ Amanda Shepard

ABOUT
THE AUTHOR

Varun Sayal is a science fiction author who has built considerable repute in the writing world within a short span of time. His science fiction works, such as *Time Crawlers* and *Demons of Time*, have been phenomenal hits on Amazon. Testimony to that fact are over five hundred positive reviews on Amazon and other platforms within just months of publishing.

www.ingramcontent.com/pod-product-compliance
Lightning Source LLC
LaVergne TN
LVHW051504170726
843492LV00002B/808